Reviews

Kudos for Jason Hess and DragonEye Publishing for another riveting edition of the Mike Taylor series, Investigation of Davis Swamp. This book is a real page turner... keeps you in suspense.. Cannot wait to see where the Mike Taylor series takes us.
Nicole Conger

~~~

I loved reading Investigation of Davis Swamp! This is a book that I couldn't put down and had to finish it in one day! This book has the perfect amount of humor mixed with suspense to make it a must read for everyone. I also loved how I was able to put myself into a visual of the scene and became a part of the story throughout the book!
Amy Lefler

~~~

Reviews

<u>Other books available</u>

Paratales- Paranormal Short stories

~~~

So You Want To Be a Ghost Hunter

~~~

Ghost Hunted: The Beginning of the Mike Taylor Series –
Book 1

~~~

Investigation of Davis Swamp: The Mike Taylor Series –
Book 2

~~~

More to come….

Investigation of Davis Swamp

The Mike Taylor Series
Book 2

By
Jason Hess and
K. W. Kirkland

Edited by
LK Kelley

Published By DragonEye Publishing

Investigation of Davis Swamp: The Mike Taylor Series, Book 2, by Jason Hess and K. W. Kirkland
Copyright © 2016, by. Jason Hess and K. W. Kirkland

Edited by LK Kelley
Cover by Suzanna Birch

Published by, DragonEye Publishing

First Edition:
First Printing October 7, 2016

ISBN 13: 978-1-61500-133-0   (Paperback)
ISBN 13: 978-1-61500-135-4   (EPub Ebook)
ISBN 13: 978-1-61500-163-7   (PDF)

Library of Congress Control Number: 2016954485

Publisher info. Contact
DragonEye Publishing
753 Linden Place, Unit A
Elmira, New York, 14901 USA

Website: DragonEyePublishers.com
Orders@DragonEyePublishers.com

Foreword

I had an opportunity to sit down and do something that I was a bit shy about doing and did not have the confidence to do on my own. Jason asked me to help with this book.

He is a seasoned paranormal investigator and he knows all the different aspects of his hobby. But when it came to doing another fictional book he was getting a little lost in spicing things up. And that's where I came in.

The second book in the Mike Taylor series, takes us on a journey to the south. To a swamp where Mike and his buddy Kevin try to help out an older lady. Mrs. Davis is a widow who owns property on the swamp, and some weird twist and turns so some of the crazy things paranormal investigators get into.

After the first book where Mikes team were lost Kevin helps spark the love of the paranormal that Mike once had.

A young lawyer named Jonathan Johnson finds a case down south and gets the boys onboard. They head down with their gear and dive in head first, even the reluctant Mike.

Once again this story shows knowledge that Jason has of the paranormal and legends. As well as his twisted sense of humor that we all close to him know.

No matter how serious any situation can get in the book as in real life Jason throws something into the mix to make even the Pope smile.

I fell luck to be able to lend a hand and even luckier to get credit for it. Hopefully Jason will do the same in the future with me.

K. W. Kirkland

Dedicated to all of the ones I love

My wife, my kids, all my family and friends everywhere. Thank you all for being in my life.

With the new day comes new strength and new thoughts.

Eleanor Roosevelt

1

As I sit here, I wonder what could have been. I slowly raise my head, and look into the closet where her clothes still hang. Although she has been gone for six months, I feel like she could walk through the door to our bedroom any minute. The reason she died is because of my selfish need to find answers, which stemmed from my greed. Now, more questions are running through my head like lightning bolts from a thunder storm.

My name is Mike Taylor, and I don't know what I am anymore. Years ago, I started a paranormal group called V.G.H. (Virginia Ghost Hunters), and made the mistake of accepting the wrong client. Six months ago, I received a call from someone, who we thought was a woman in need. Instead, everything turned around, and we became the hunted. I lost friends, and even more Samantha – the woman I truly loved.

I spent time in jail that night along with another member who also survived, not only for killing my girlfriend, but both of us were accused for the disappearance of the rest of the group. Eventually, all charges were dropped, and I was cleared of all charges due to lack of evidence. But this all still haunts me.

I am still friends with the last member of our group, Kevin. He and I rarely talk about that night, which left us both injured. He had a broken leg while I had a snapped arm and cracked ribs. While that pain went away, the emotional scars will never leave me.

With a degree in business, I have sold cars in the past, but now, I am a clerk at a video rental store. I ran through a trust fund from my grandfather, most of it having been depleted since I got out of jail. But, I am lucky. At least, I still have my house. I was afraid that would have to go to pay some lawyer to represent me in trial. One lawyer named Jonathan R. Johnson jumped at the chance to do so. He recently had graduated law school, and passed the Bar exam. He offered to defend me at no cost simply because he thought it would help make a name for himself. And, we were exonerated. He even escorted us to the house as it was being torn down where everything had happened. That just added to the mystery, because our equipment was there. Kev and I grabbed it, before it was gone, but there was still no sign of our friends who had been lost in the house. As it was knocked down, I was hit with mixed emotions. One that I knew the house would never trap anyone again, and two the sadness for the loss of our group.

Alone, I returned to my empty house. The house was filled with its own ghosts – the ones that will always remind me of her. They will never go away, but then, I do not want them to disappear.

I turn my head to look at the clock. I sigh. I was expected to be at work in thirty minutes. So, I finally stood, took a deep breath, and exited my bedroom. As I walk downstairs, I wonder why I was spared? I guess God has a purpose for me – to rent bad movies at a low, low price, and remember the popcorn.

Twenty minutes later, I jump out of my POS cargo van, and head inside for another thrilling day. Nothing is more interesting than a woman trying to explain why a rental came back late, or hearing the plot of a movie I hated ten years ago.

As the night went on Kevin came in to see me. Believe it or not this was the bright point of my night. See Kevin is a unique person that has been stuck in the days of hair bands.

"Dude, what are you doing after work?" said Kevin.

"Nothing. Just going to go home and crash," I told him.

"Well, grab a flick, and come over to my place for beer and zza."

First, the pizza is pizza, and it's probably a frozen one. Another thing is his place consists of a one room studio apartment with one chair, a bed, and a sixty inch projection TV. Also, the sheets on the bed had to be white once but now seem to be an off gray, and they just might fall apart if they were washed. And, finally, the place smelled like dog crap, which is understandable. Kev cleans dog cages at a pet store.

"I will grab a movie, and we can order a pizza from my house. You just bring what you want, OK?"

"Cool," Kevin replied. "Why don't we say like eleven? That cool?"

"Cool."

"OK. See you then," he said, adding, "Oh! And, you also should check your messages once in a while. Jon Jon has been trying to get a hold of you."

Kevin left the store, and I tried to think who in the hell Jon Jon was. And, then it hit me. Our lawyer, Jonathan, but why is he calling now? The case is over.

I guess I will find out when I get home. This, thank God, is soon since we close in a few minutes. So, I better go grab a movie, before I lock up.

2

Well, it's now eleven thirty...and no Kevin. I walked over to the answering machine, and started to listen to the many messages. Most of them I just deleted, until I found one of ten messages from Jonathan.

"Mike, it's Jonathan Johnson. I need to talk to you as soon as possible. One of my new clients has said that she is losing her house in Georgia. They have twenty acres, and she told me that her husband hid money somewhere on them. But, here's the thing. She also told me that there is swamp land, and she is afraid to enter it! And, why? Because, his "ghost" prevents her from doing it! So, she has made a deal, and asked me to relay it to you. She said that if you will find that money for her in the swamp, he will give you ten percent. Please, let me know what you think."

I backed away from the table and the answering machine as if a snake was about to strike! I swore that I would give up all this paranormal shit. But, it's a passion with me, and hard to not pursue it. I don't know what to do.

Seconds later, the front door crashed open, scaring the shit out of me! Kevin walks in carrying a beer in one hand complete with a smirk on his face. I should really lock my door at all times! That's my bad.

We ordered a large pizza with everything except, as Kevin put it, "those little fishy things". While waiting for it to be delivered, we started to watch one of those action movies with Steven Segal. Unfortunately, Kevin kept talking, so watching it was almost next to impossible.

"By the way. I talked to Jon today. Did you get his messages?"

"Yeah," I said. "He offered me a job, but I think I am going to pass."

"Dude! I *need* you to go with me."

My head turn so quick I am lucky it didn't fly off, and into the TV! What did he mean "go with him"? Did Jonathan talk to him first, and Kevin actually accepted it? This isn't good! Kevin is a good cameraman, but as an investigator, he is weak.

"Kev, you know I gave all that paranormal stuff up! It's my past, and I just can't go back."

"Now, you don't want to help people plagued by paranormal activity? Did you, or did you not, tell me that you got into this line of work, because you wanted to help people? Telling people that the noise they hear at night is their water heater, or that the voices they hear is really nothing more than their neighbors talking loud, does *not* constitute helping them!" Kevin exclaimed, then, continues. "This old lady needs our help, man! You can't turn her down!"

"Absolutely not! We did all of that, and just *look* what happened. look at all we lost! Think about who *I lost!* No way will I you or me in danger, again! This sounds almost like the last time, and I can't do it!"

The doorbell rang, luckily, and it stopped the conversation. It was the pizza guy, and after I paid him, I closed the door. The rest of the night, Kev and I didn't talk to each other that much, and he left around two in the morning. I know he was mad, but he will get over it. I just hope he doesn't go down to Georgia alone.

After I cleaned up the mess, I went upstairs to bed. After brushing my teeth, I walked into my room, and climbed into bed. Sleeping alone in a king size bed is weird now. I still sleep on my side of the bed, and always think that she would be there when I woke, but she is never there, of course. I rolled to my side, and saw a light coming from under the bedroom door.

I sat up and looked harder. I know I turned off all the lights, and I was just wondering where it was coming from, when the light disappeared. I lay back down, thinking maybe it was a passing car or something else. Again, the light appeared and disappeared once again. OK, now I got to check this out.

I carefully opened the door, and walked into the hall. No light, just plain darkness. So, I walked to the edge of the stairs, and still saw nothing. Scratching my head in confusion, I dismissed it, and went back into bed. This time, I closed my eyes so I couldn't see if it appeared, again..

Around four o'clock, I was awoken by a voice. It was very familiar; a voice I had heard many times. It sounded like Carrie. Carrie and her husband, Mark, were part of V.G.H., and had died by falling through the railing on the second floor. She was the group's sensitive, and had helped Sam and me.

Raising my head, I didn't see anyone in my room. But, I heard the voice, again. Was I dreaming? Or worse? I had become nuts, and I would just wait for those guys in the white coats with the big net to arrive!

"*Mike! Wake up, Mike!*"

"Carrie? Is that you?"

"*Mike, it is me, and don't worry you're not crazy.*"

OK, now, this voice is telling me that it could read my mind, too. ThenI realized that as sensitive, Carrie was able to communicate with people that have passed. What if it can work the other way too? I am about as sensitive as a rock.

"Mike, when we started this group, it was with a purpose. Now, you are going back on your word! You once said that we would never turn anyone down if there was something that needed investigating! You need to go with Kevin, and help this lady! Don't even think about what happened before, could happen, again. This was what you were meant to do!"

"Carrie, I can't take that chance, and I won't do it. What if…."

The voice interrupted me.

"Mike, I told you that I would always be with you. Now go to sleep, and when you awake in the morning, do what you promised!"

"No. I can't."

There was no answer. The brief time she was here was enough for me. I always had trusted her, so tomorrow, I guess I will call Jonathan, and see what I can do even though I'm not too happy about it. And, it is what I do – go to places that are haunted to help people and to record what I find. With this, my first task was to figure out where the old man had buried his family's money. People have a lot of faith in what we do, but I don't agree. Anyway, it's time that I suck it up and try.

3

I awoke to nothing, as usual, but now, I have a purpose. Its nine twenty in the morning, and I feel more energized than I have in months! As I pulled on a pair of pants, I started to plan my day. But first? I need coffee...a *lot* of coffee.

I poured the water into the coffee pot, and began to brew the first cups. Then, I sat down at my small kitchen table. looking out the window across the table, I noticed I had not seen a day so bright in ages! Not a cloud outside, and there's a squirrel climbing the tree in my neighbors yard.

It's funny how depression can cloud your mind. You never notice the things around you, or the things that can be important to you. At least coffee clears the mind!

As I poured my first cup of coffee, my phone rang. It was Kevin, so I answered. I told him that I was going to set up a meeting with Jonathan, and I wanted him to come with me. Kevin was ecstatic, and told me he would come right over.

I laid the phone down, and sipped my coffee, spitting it out just as quick. Worst coffee I ever tasted! It was bitter and hot, and nothing like I ever tasted! looking over to the counter, and I realized that what I made was a Turkish blend! Well, now, I knew why it was on sale. I took another sip,   walked through the kitchen, then upstairs to change my clothes.

When I came back down, I noticed that all the equipment was still where I had dropped it when I finally brought it home a month ago! There was an additional large pile of bags and cases by the wall in the foyer.

BANG!!!

Well, it's obvious that Kevin's here. I walked over to the door I had finally locked, and opened it for him. He stood there rubbing his forehead, and I guess that is what hit the door. He came in and headed for the kitchen. I poured a cup of coffee for him as he sat down. Kevin was dressed up today in a button down shirt, jeans, old tennis shoes, and an AC/DC hat. Yes. This is dressed up for him.

"Well we are going to be at Jonathan's office at eleven. I don't know what is going to happen, or how long it will take."

"Bro, I don't care. I just missed this shit. I can't wait till we hit the road," Kevin said. "It's about time that we do something instead of sitting around drinking all the time! That is so boring. Besides, all that beer is making me look fat."

It wasn't the beer that made him look fat; it was his fat that made him look fat. He never was in excellent shape, but for a chubby guy he could run like a gazelle…no a deer…wait...I know! An elephant. I would tease him, but you know that he is a good guy.

"Well, I wish I felt the same way buddy," I said. "I am a little scared 'bout the whole thing."

"We got to move on bro," said Kevin. "We need to open our wings and fly."

OK. He was trying to sound like a motivational speaker, but he sounds more like a cheap comic at a two bit comedy club. But, at least he tries. And, that's more than I have been doing recently. It's the moment that I thought that Kevin, of all people, could inspire me to get out of my funk.

"Dude we can overcome all odds and come out on top!"

"Kev. OK. You can stop, now. I said I would do it, but fear isn't something that will go away that fast. But, I am working on it. Come on drink the rest of your coffee. We got to go."

And, on that note, he slid his chair back, stood at attention, turned, took a step, and what else? He tripped, of course. He fell straight down, landing on his hands and knees. But, like a true comedian, he popped right back up and walked to the door.

Smiling and shaking my head in amusement, I grabbed my jacket, cell phone, and followed him out the door. Leave it to Kevin to do something to break tension. The thing is he does it without knowing. His timing is the worst, but he keeps me smiling.

Jumping into the van, I drove downtown to the lawyer's office. It's not that far, and we are not late, but I was speeding, because Kevin was playing the air drums again to an old rock song. It's really annoying, so the quicker we get there, he'll have to stop.

When we got into Jonathan's meeting room, I thought it would be similar to I had seen on TV. A large, long, dark wood table with six chairs, book cases filled with hundreds of law books. And, a scenic view from a window where the drapes could be drawn.

But, that isn't what I saw. He had a card table and folding chairs. Not even one book case dotted the room, but he did have a few books in boxes. He must be just starting out, I thought. Decorating costs money.

Just as Kevin and I sat down, Jonathan walked into the room, carrying a file folder in one hand, and he shook our hands with the other. He started to explain everything. All that legal mumble jumble is boring as hell!

"The point is that at one time, they had money. However, she says she knows where it is, but she can't get to it, because his ghost is stopping her from getting to it. She is very scared, and foreclosing proceeds begin next week. So, I know you guys are ghost hunters, and…."

"Dude, we are *paranormal investigators*. We are the rock stars of the haunting world," Kevin explained with a straight face. Can I call a mistrial now?

"I am sorry," Jonathan continued. "What we need is some evidence that the money is on the property, and then we can postpone all the loss she may accrue."

"So, what? You want us to go in and prove there are ghosts there, so they won't foreclose?" I asked. "That seems a little strange. Why would they hold off on everything, because of a haunting?"

"No Mike. We need to see if the "ghost" is real enough to show you where the money might be hidden, and if it is the spirit of her late husband, maybe he will lead you to the place he buried it."

"This is a long shot. Ghosts just don't act on a whim, and getting advice or directions from them are next to impossible. We might be lucky enough to record a voice, or maybe capture an orb. But, asking them to lead us to a treasure is most doubtful."

"Well, we need to see if this long shot will pay off. She agreed to pay you ten percent of what is found, and I will be paying your way. What do you have to lose?"

At that point, I looked at Kevin who was staring off into space, and asked him if he wanted to do this. And, that was the most ridiculous Questions that I have asked in a long time. But I had to know. And, of course he agreed. I reckon we're going to Georgia.

4

We planned to leave the next day, so, last night, I checked out all the equipment we would need, and made sure we had batteries – and coffee that I normally drank. After getting very little sleep, I drank my coffee. Kevin had said that he would be at my place around nine this morning, which on "Kevin-time" really meant nine thirty. I looked at my watch. It was five to nine, now. So, when there was a knock at my front door, I was surprised to find that it was Jonathan, and he was carrying a bag. OK, I admit it. I am confused.

"Hey Jonathan you going somewhere?"

"I am going with you," said Jonathan. "Remember, I am paying your way."

"Jonathan, my van only has two seats. There is just no room for you."

"Well...would all your stuff fit in my Escalade?"

Well, he did have a point. I mean, going from my POS to a Caddy...? Nope. No contest!

"Sure it will. We are only taking a couple bags. You know, just the hand-held stuff."

"Then, there's no problem. I will throw my things in the back of my truck. Then, I'll come back, and help you with your bags."

Jonathan and I loaded up his truck, while we waited for Kevin. About a half-hour later, he arrived, got out of his car, and slammed the door – twice, three times, until on the forth slam, it closed. He needs a new car more than I do.

"Dude…Jon-Jon! So, what's shakin' bros?"

Well, that's about as welcome a greeting one gets from Kevin. He never seems to let anything bother him, and he always has a great outlook on life. It's one of the few things that I admire about him. There's a lot I wish I could change about him, but his positive attitude? Never.

"Kev, Jonathan is coming with us. We are taking his truck."

"Whoa! We're goin' cruisin' in style? Love it, Dude!"

Kevin threw his garbage away, stashed his duffle bag in the truck, and then, he jumped in the back seat. Jonathan and I looked at each other, trying to stifle our laughs, and followed him to the Escalade.

Virginia to Georgia is a really a long ride. But, at least it's comfortable, and the radio sounded great. Then, as Jonathan turned the radio down so we could talk, we heard some strange things coming out of the backseat.

"*Mumble, mumble...*and things that fly... *Mumble, mumble.*"

Is Kevin talking in his sleep? It's always hard to talk when someone talks in their sleep. But, even though, we tried, what came was understandable enough. He was singing?

"But I couldn't believe it,
I just had to find out for myself,
And, I couldn't conceive it, 'Cause I never would have listened to nobody else.
And, I couldn't believe it.
I just had to find out for myself
there's something's in this world you just can't explain."

Oh, man! He's off key, but he is entertaining.
"Kevin what are you singing?"
"Hmmm?" he muttered.
"I said, what are you singing?"
"Oh. 'The Legend of Wooley Swamp'. It's a classic, you know, and it kinda fits what we are doing."
"And, just how does it fit, Kev?"
"Hell. In the song, the dude buried his money in coffee cans. And, now he haunts the grounds where they are buried."
OK. He was right, but I can't stand listening to him sing anymore! Hopefully, it is a short set, and we can be done with it. So, Jonathan

and I tried to continue our conversation over his singing.

"Let me get this straight. As I take it from what you have told me, this lady, Mrs. Mary Ellen Davis, lost her husband two years ago. He was a true back woods redneck, never trusting the government or banks. He was also a fisherman selling his catch to restaurants, and such. And, he was good at it, too."

"So far, so good," I told him.

"OK. Mr. Davis was a real tight wad, and never spent too much of his money. He would fish or hunt for his meat, trade for other food and needs like clothing and supplies. But, since he didn't spend the money, he would bury the money on the property. The bad thing is he never told anyone where it was. Not even his wife. "So then, she goes out to the swampy area to see if she could find some of that money to save her property, and gets run off by something she can't see. This poor woman is scared and has nowhere to go."

"That's about right," I agreed.

"See bros? Just like the song!"

Fourteen hours later, we were almost there. Driving another thirty minutes, we were bushed, and knew we needed to catch some sleep for the night. So, Jonathan pulled into a motel, and got a couple rooms. The Hilton, it was not, but it will do for the night.

5

Kevin and I shared a room, and about ten minutes after we settled into the room, he was out like a light, snoring louder than anything I have ever heard.

"Oh, great," I muttered sarcastically, my voice a whisper. "This is really going to be a *good* night."

Not only was he doing a good imitation of a walrus mating call, but I'm sinking in a hole in the bed, and I just can't get out of it!

Suddenly, I could see a beautiful woman that stopped me in my tracks. It was Samantha, standing at the edge of my bed. I thought I would never see her again.

I jumped out of bed, reaching for her as I walked. I grabbed, and pulled her into me in a tight embrace. looking into her eyes, a tear ran down my face.

"I miss you Sam," I said with sadness in my voice.

She smiled, and leaned into me, kissing me. This is what I have missed the most – the touch of her soft lips against mine. looking at me, she just started to speak, when...

...Buzzzzzzzzzzz...

I jerked awake, frantically looking for Sam. "Damn!"

It was just a dream! A dream that would never end. And, it would be a haunting from a bad memory that will be with me forever. Now, I look at a large man's butt-crack in the bed across from me. I almost snarled at the unfairness of my lot in life.

Sunlight brOKe through the drapes, and I knew I had to get up, but waking up from the dream will never get easier. I always have dreams about Sam.

"Kev….wake up."

All he did was cover his head with a pillow. Now, I finally understand why he is always late. It might take an hour to get him out of the bed! So, instead of trying to talk to him, I hit him with a pillow – and, a few choice words added into it, until he finally caved, and dragged himself out of the bed with a frown.

I padded into the bathroom, and looked in the mirror. Nothing different today, I guess. I closed the door, and could hear Kevin making noise as he turned on the TV.

"Dude, we are leaving in a half hours, so you don't really have time for the TV!"

He gave me a "you really know how to ruin a morning" look, tossed down the remote without turning off the TV (a defiant action on his part,

I'm sure), and walked into the bathroom. While I dressed, my mind ran over the case. Why would a man, who didn't trust banks, have a loan on his property? This didn't make much sense to me. And even more...why would he hide his money from his own family in the first place?

Kevin came back into the room, and pulled on the same clothes that he wore yesterday. He had a bag with him, and looked a bit smaller today. I gave him the skinny of what our plan of the day was.

"OK. Today, we are going to meet Mrs. Davis, and hear from her first-hand," I told him. This is an investigator's way of being able to get a read on a person. We have to determine if she is telling us the facts. "Then, we will be checking out some of the land that is in question."

The whole interview process is needed before going in to any investigation. Experience has taught me that this is critical. We can take some base line readings on the electromagnetic fields that are present, and this is much easier to do in Daylight. Sometimes, both weather and temperature may change this.

I grabbed my bag, and motioned to Kevin that it was time to go. I opened the door, and Jonathan was standing by his truck – with coffee. "Thank God for coffee!" I told him, taking the steaming cup that he held out for me.

Taking it, I got into the car, and the other two followed my lead.

6

After a brief conversation about the case so we were all on the same page, we all piled into the Escalade, and headed to the house. Kevin sat there with his bag to his side. I am really wondering what's in inside it, now. Jonathan followed the directions given by our GPS, and said that we should be there in about twenty minutes.

The view out the window was absolutely beautiful! I mean, it's not like this in Virginia, but it's a different type of beautiful. In Virginia, it's clean and the wooded area seemed quite uniform. Here in Georgia, though, the swampy land gave a different perspective altogether. Long moss hanging down from the trees, draped over them, while hiding all of its secrets. It was truly beautiful and mysterious at the same time.

A little time passed, and we were getting close to our destination. The wooded swamp started getting thicker, and signs of civilization got smaller. It had been at least ten minutes since we had passed the last house.

"Turn right, now," said the disembodied, GPS voice.

Turning as we were told, we turned onto a gravel road. It wasn't a very good road, nor was it very wide. Jonathan had to keep swerving to miss holes, or things lying in the middle of the road.

We came to a line of trees where the road split between them. We took the road on the right, and headed drove about a hundred feet, only stopping at a rickety old shack that loomed in front of us. It looked as if it had a tin roof on the wooden frame. We couldn't believe this! How could anyone possibly live here?

We thought the GPS was wrong, so Jonathan started to back up the truck to backtrack, when a little woman walked out of the door. She was, maybe five foot tall, looking for all the world as if she was three hundred years old! Surprised, Jonathan threw the truck in park, and opened the door. I was looking around, and all the redneck jokes came to mind in that instant. All that was needed was some guy playing a banjo on the front porch. Both Kevin and I opened the doors, and stepped out of the Escalade.

We joined Jonathan as we walked up to him, while he and the old lady stopped in mid conversation as we approached.

"And...this is Mike and Kevin, who are paranormal investigators, and they are here to help you." Jonathan continued, "Is there a place we can all sit and talk?"

"Why, y'all come right on in!" said the old lady. "Are you thirsty? Would y'all like a glass of lemonade if you are."

"That would be nice Mrs. Davis. Thank you. Please, lead the way," Jonathan answered.

The old lady smiled and started to walk towards the shack, picking up a basket as she went. She let us to the back of the shack, where I thought we were going. Instead, a beautiful split level house rose in front of us about two hundred feet on the other side of the shack, which was completely hidden by the shack, and the trees surrounding it! The shack looked as if it had built prior to the civil war, but this house couldn't be over ten or twenty years old. I was truly confused.

She led us through the doors, and into a small entrance. To the right, was the living room and straight ahead was the kitchen, where she was leading us. It was nothing really fancy, but it was comfortable. After motioning us to sit down at the table, we began the investigation.

"Mrs. Davis can you please tell me everything that has been happening here?" I asked the old lady as she sat down in the fourth chair.

"Well, it all seemed to start about ten years ago. Lou...that's my husband, and his brother Clay. ran a fishin' business. Lou would go out and catch the catfish, and then, Clay would sell them to restaurants and markets. They were making a lot of money, and wanted to expand. So, Clay took a loan out on the property. They bought some boats, and hired some guys from town." Mrs. Davis took a drink of her lemonade, and continued. "We were able to build this house with the money we were making, and everything seemed to be going good."

"Then, one day Lou and Clay had a huge fight, and Clay left." She took another drink, and told us more. "You see, Lou just couldn't run the business alone. Clay did all the business end, and Lou fished. My Lou just loved fishin', you see. But, the business started to decline. We lost people that worked for us, and Lou started to worry. So, instead of puttin' the money in the bank, he would bury it somewhere. He didn't trust the bank, 'cause he thought they were stealin' his money. But, the truth was, they were actually payin' off the loan, and some other bills. Well, soon, people stopped buyin' as many fish from him, and he began to lose money. Pretty soon, he wasn't bringin' home any money. Then one day, he went out fishin', but just didn't come back. I called the sheriff, and he came out to search for him. A day later, they found his body in the swamp. He was dead."

She picked up a napkin, and wiped a tear from her face. Then, she looked up to the ceiling, and Kevin looked up, too. I don't have a clue why he did it, but he stopped after I nudged him.

"So, what happened," Jonathan asked.

"Oh. Well, it seemed he had a heart attack, and fell into the swamp. Lou was a great swimmer, even though he was seventy two. But, they say he was dead by the time he hit the water."

"At the funeral, Clay came back. He told me he would help me out what really happened. But, instead of takin' the business, and keepin' it goin', he sold it off to some city guy. I didn't see any money from that deal at all. Then he started bringin' in all these machines, knockin' down trees, and diggin' holes. See, he knows Lou buried money just like his pa and grandpa did. So, I decided to start lookin' for the money myself. The bank wants to take all our land away! I need that money to pay them! Clay doesn't care about me at all! He just wants to find the moneym" she told us.

"Mrs. Davis...is there any proof that your husband, did bury that money on the property?" asked Jonathan. I was taking notes. Sometimes, having someone else doing the questioning helps me to take notes, and it lets me concentrate on the story.

"Well, I saw him go out to the swamp with a week's earnings. He just had to be burying it. I tried to go out there, and find it, but every time I do, I hear voices telling me to go away, and I...see things."

"Well Mrs. Davis, what we do is document paranormal activity. Then, we analyze it to see if there is any spirit activity. We are not treasure hunters. I think that you contacted the wrong people," I told her. "I am very sorry to waste your time, but I do not feel we can be of any help to you."

"If you can tell me the voices I hear, and the thing I see is my Lou, then I wouldn't be afraid to go out there. I couldn't be afraid of my own husband."

"Is there family that would take you in if anything happens?" asked Jonathan. "I mean, I might be able to hold the bank for a few days, but just in case, do you have somewhere to go."

"Well, the good Lord never blessed us with children. I guess maybe I could go to my sister's place. She lives in Atlanta."

"Mike will you please try and see if you can find anything? In the meantime, I will see if I can contact the bank and get a few more days," asked Jonathan.

I agreed, against my better judgment, and stood, nudging Kevin. We walked out of the house, and back to the truck. I really hate knowing that this poor woman is putting complete faith in something as farfetched as this. But, we need to try. Hopefully, we might find something.

7

Kevin leaned up against the Escalade and set out a sigh. He really gets bored easily, and loses his train of thought even faster. He looked around him.

I opened the tailgate, and grabbed a few pieces of equipment we would be needing. We didn't need much, since we would be outside, and we can't use everything we brought with us anyway. So right now a camera, voice recorder, and an EMF meter is all we're going to take. We are only going through a quick walk, not a full investigation.

Getting base readings are really important. If we have a consistent reading, we have a change that tells us that something is not right. Especially when we get a high electromagnetic spike, and there is no electricity in a swamp. We should not get a reading there.

So I grabbed it all and handed the voice recorder and emf meter to Kevin. I will take pictures and try to get a feel for the area. This is the first time we have ever investigated a swamp. Cemeteries were hard enough with all the sounds around us, now I am going to have to listen to all these new sounds that I am not use to.

"OK, Kev. Let's head in and see what's going on."

"Dude! This place is creepy as hell! I hope we don't run into Bigfoot or something!"

I rolled my eyes at him.

"Bigfoot is in the northwest of the country, Kev...not in Georgia! But..." I said, rubbing my chin pretending to think, and pursing my lips. "...you know? I can't remember where that swamp ape is from. I'm sure that won't be a problem."

After a quick look from Kevin that resembled horror, we walked closer to the edge of the woods. Once we entered, the trees began to smother the sunlight, and were swallowing up any other light. Just a tiny pinprick of light was trickling through the dense leaves above us, while long strands of hanging moss on the tree limbs were taking care of any remaining light.

Five minutes after entering the woods, the ground begins to get soft, and each step on the squishing ground means we are getting a little closer to the swamp. The humidity is so high, I don't know how people can stand it I n full blown summer. We are barely in springtime, and I am sweating up a storm! Kev has sweat pouring off his face, and looking at his shirt, I held out hope that he had brought more clothes.

A little longer into our walk, and we saw open water. It doesn't look deep at all. A small pier with a green flat bottom boat tied to it, stuck straight out in front of us. Birds and other types of wild life start to warn other animals that humans were around them. Stumps and tree limbs littered the water giving an eerie, but serene view.

"I'm going to start snapping pictures. Why don't you start taking the EMF readings?" I told Kevin.

"No problem, Dude. Audio too?" he asked me.

"I don't think so. The birds might contaminate the audio. Tonight, it will be a must, but not right now."

Kevin gave me a thumbs up, and shoved the voice recorder into his pocket, and turned on the meter. He started to walk slowly, seeing if there are any disturbances in the area. I, in turn, started to snap pictures. When I do this tonight, I can match up the pictures to see if there are any differences between the pictures. Also, at night a flash may highlight something and it could be considered paranormal even though it's not.

There is an area across the water from the boat that looked like a bit weird as if someone made it that way for some kind of rituals. Weird, just plain weird, and its nothing I have ever seen before!

I zoomed into the area with my camera to try to take a closer look, but it was just a little too far. Maybe, when I download the pictures onto my laptop, I could enlarge it enough so that I could see the area, before jumping to any conclusions.

Just as I finished the last of the three pictures I wanted, I heard Kevin scream.

"Crocagator…um allidile…ah, hell! What ever it is, it's after me!"

Kevin is no small man. But, he was hauling ass right past me, and to a tall tree with a lower branch. He jumped, and grabbed the branch, trying to pull himself up the tree fast.

"Kevin? Kevin! What in the hell? What did you see?" I screamed at him.

He pulled himself over the branch, straddling it like a horse. He was trying to catch his breath, when I walked over to him. He waved his hand at me, signaling, me to wait a moment.

"There was a fucking alligator, or crocodile in the water! And, hell! It looked hungry!"

"Don't you think if there were alligators out her, Mrs. Davis would have warned us? So, get down here!"

"No way, Dude. Maybe you will be skinny enough, so they won't see you as a snack! I am a freaking buffet to them!" Kevin squawked. "And, I ain't getting out of this tree till I know that thing is gone! It's like twenty feet long, so I can see it coming from up here," he panted in fear.

"Ummm...Mike? Do you know if they could climb trees?"

OK, now I have to find this gator, and see if it's real or not. So, I backtracked his steps, and started to walk. The good thing is that since the ground was so soft, I could just follow his footprints. After a couple of minutes, I could see where he had stopped.

I stopped to look around...and..there it was! At least twenty feet long and about three feet wide! I saw it bobbing up in the water, and then going down under only to bob back up to the surface. I took the camera, and starting taking pictures. This thing was freaking huge, but I don't think we were in any danger, so I turned and walked back to Kevin.

8

I trudged forward with a smirk on my face, and approached Kevin. Yes. He was still up in the tree. And, his face looked as if some big lizard that destroyed Tokyo was going to eat him!

"Kev, come down!" I told him.

"Dude, as long as 'it's' out there, I won't be! Let me say it one more time! I. Ain't. Going *Nowhere*!"

"Oh, for the love of…. It was a *tree*, Kevin! You know, as in *t r e e?*" I spelled it out for him. "There is *no* alligator! Come down...please!" I added.

Now, Kevin isn't the brightest bulb on the tree, but he knows I wouldn't bullshit him. His face still wary, he started down the tree. One foot hit the ground...then the next...followed by his his butt, back, and head. I tried not to laugh, but it was just too hilarious!

Kevin stood and brushed off his clothes. He walked over to me looked me dead in the face, and said, "What's up?"

That only made me laugh that much harder as I grabbed my side, because it was hurting. As soon as I was able to talk, and it took a while, I told him that we needed to check the trees on the other side of the swamp.

"I can't see any other way across the swamp except to take the boat," I said.

After all, it has to belong to Mrs. Davis, because it's on her property. Kevin had no problem with it, so we walked to the boat. When we reached the boat, we looked inside, then looked at each with scowls, then held our noses. It stunk! Inside the boat there were bird droppings, fish scales, and what looked like a small, folding shovel. As dirty as it was, we still needed to make our way across the swamp, so we got into it, and Kevin rowed across the swamp very fast, and without a problem. The truth is that If I was rowing? Well, we would be going in circles for a half hour. Later, I found out that he didn't really believe that there was no gator, but just didn't want to look like a wimp.

When we reached the other side, we pulled out the equipment, and started taking EMF readings, and finished by taking pictures. Almost immediately. we came across a huge EMF spike. With no power lines, and no electricity anywhere around, we couldn't explain it. Then, just as fast as it came, it disappeared.

We circled around the area, and every once in a while, we would get another spike. Usually, that spike was somewhere outside of the circle near the trees. There was an EMF field higher than we ever recorded in the exact middle.

looking towards the center, we noticed that the ground was very uneven, and the highest point was in the middle. It's not natural, and more than likely, it was done by man. But who would have done it? And, another thing that was odd. We didn't hear any wildlife at all, and I didn't think about it until just now. It was a little spooky, but we have to keep going despite it.

"Kevin? Do you still have the voice recorder with you?"

"Yeah. Want me to start rolling?"

"I think that would be a good idea. It's quieter over here, so we won't have any real problem in reviewing it this afternoon."

As Kevin hit record on the voice recorder, I took a few more pictures. A paranormal investigator always takes multiple photos of the scene. Then, we check to see if there's anything on the small screen before moving on to another picture. However, something had caught my attention on this one.

Every once in a while, we might catch an orb, it is usually some dust or a bug. On this photo, though, I saw a wispy fog. There should be no fog at this time of day, and neither Kevin nor I smoke. I quickly snapped three more pictures in rapid succession. Unfortunately, I was unable to capture it, again. Kevin knew I caught something, and he started to walk toward the area where I was focused. About ten feet from the trees, the EMF meter started going nuts!

"There's a huge temperature drop!" Kevin told me.

In order for a spirit to emerge, it needs energy to manifest itself, and with it, creates an electro magnetic field – or EMF for short. The theory is that when a spirit appears, it draws out the heat, and thus, a cold area is created.

I needed to go check it out for myself. After Kevin handed me the EMF, I saw that Kevin was right! It had to be at least ten degrees colder in an area that encompassed three feet in diameter. There was absolutely no wind, and no reason for it to be happening. We made a note on the voice recorder, and followed with a few pictures, too.

After a few minutes the cold spot disappeared, and was replaced by the muggy, hot air as if the cold had never happened. I figured that it was time we should start heading back, when I looked down, and saw something shining back at me. I leaned down, and reached for it. Why would someone throw a mason jar lid into the swamp? I started to brush away some of the dirt, and more of the jar appeared. Kevin saw I was digging up something and joined me in cleaning it away. As the dirt was cleared away, we could see the contents of the jar. It was cash, and it was a lot of it!

Maybe this is the money Mr. Davis buried? But, was there more here? We continued to dig with our hands, trying to find another jar or two. Then, the air, once again, started to change.

"Mike, go now, you have to go NOW!" Carrie's voice echoed through my head. I looked around me, realized that not only had the air become heavy, but it began to darken around me.

"Kev, head to the boat! We need to go – now!" I exclaimed, echoing Carrie's demand.

"But, Dude. We are getting hits everywhere!" said Kevin in surprise.

"I don't care! We will come back later but we have to go!"

Under protest, Kevin finally agreed and we headed for the boat. Once Kevin was in it, I pushed the boat into the water, before I jumped in it. I looked back towards the circle of trees and sat down. The whole area began to darken even more, and it became harder to see. I still, to this day, can't explain why there was so much urgency for us to leave. Once we stumbled into our room, we set up our equipment to look over the pictures and audio that we had taken earlier.

9

When we reached the pier, we tied the boat to it. Then, Kevin climbed out of it, leaving me looking back to where we had come. I swear, I could see movement in the pitch black. I took a few more snapshots, and stepped out of the boat.

Walking back through the woods to the house, we saw Jonathan standing by his truck. And, the closer we got to him, we noticed that Jon had a smile on his face. Now, what was that all about?

"What's up Jon Jon? I gotta question. Dude. Are there gators around here?" questioned Kevin.

"I don't know Kevin, but I will find out for you. So, find anything?"

"Well, we went across the swamp to a suspicious area," I said. "There are very high EMF spikes, and several weird things, too. The ground looks like it has been disturbed, but it was grown over with grass and brush. And, we found this..."

I showed him the jar, and he gasps. He turned it in his hand, examining as if it were an archeology artifact. Jonathan turned back to me.

"You actually found some money?"

"Yeah, Jon. Maybe even more. But after we unearthed it, darkness fell on us, like a shroud! I felt like we needed to leave, before we could look for anything else. There is something else there, too. And, I am not talking about buried money, but something protecting it. It doesn't seem like it's a dark entity, but it sure doesn't want anyone else hanging around, either! We also need to go over these pictures and audio, before I could be definite. I don't want to scare Mrs. Davis, and present her with something that isn't really there." I continued, "So, I need find somewhere so that I can check all our information. OH! And, could you, maybe hit the local historical society? See if there's anything we should know?"

"OK. Mike, I could drop you guys at the motel, and then, I'll go into town," Jonathan said, as he walked to the driver's door. "I don't know about you guys, but I think this is kind of exciting."

"Dude! Hang the excitement! I'm hungry! Let's get some burgers, first!" Kevin exclaimed, climbing into the backseat." Dudes! I tell ya...I need food!"

We swung onto the highway, and the drive back seemed to go faster. But, isn't always that way? Once, Sam and I drove to the Poconos for a vacation, and on the way back, it seemed as if it took half the time to go home.

We stopped at a drive-thru hamburger joint, before going to the motel. Jonathan and I got burgers, fries, and drinks. Kevin, on the other hand, ordered half the damn menu! Now, I am starting to feel sorry for Jonathan, since he is paying for all the food.

Making it back to the hotel, we dug into the food. As I started to eat, I turned on my laptop, eager to download all the information we had.

We have an audio program, and loaded the audio from the voice recorder. We have several different programs for picture editing, too. I just really want to see that fog that I captured on a bigger screen. It should take only about half an hour to view the pictures, and only a couple hours for the audio. Kevin will look over the pictures, first, and I will view them afterward. So, it would take us maybe four or five hours, and that was our game plan for tonight.

Then, when I really started to think, I heard Carrie's voice again. In a way, I'm glad she's looking over me, but it still gave me the creeps. Also, I am really hoping that she will continue to keep the bad spirits away. She kept them away earlier, and I think she will be there for me, again. I just wish Samantha could be here too, dare to dream.

10

Through the night, Kevin and I went through the data we had collected. We listened to every second of audio, and paid attention to every picture we took. But, we came up with absolutely nothing! Not even an orb that we could argue about for an hour, then dismiss as a bug!

I thought hard, and couldn't really think of anything out of the ordinary. Well, being in a swamp is out of the ordinary, but nothing but natural sounds and feelings. That high energy spike and that cold spot that we can't really explain, and worse is that we can't really count as evidence, either. It could just possibly be that the equipment malfunctioned, and a breeze came by to help create the cold spot. It's a long shot, sure, but we always want to be precise with our claims. So, if there is any doubt about anything, then we use the old phrase – "when in doubt, throw it out".

I look over at Kevin, and notice that he is going through his "duffle" bag. Why was he trying to be so secretive about it? What *is* he doing, I don't really care much but I hope he is looking for clothes to wear tomorrow. The sweat stains on the ones he is wearing are noticeable, but tomorrow, they will have a "nice" odor to it. But, enough of the visions and smells of that one! Time to get back to work.

I continued to listen to the audio, again, only this time, I heard what might be a faint voice. I highlighted that section of audio, and made a new file. Then, I enhanced the volume. Yes! There is a voice! I have to clean it up, and erase some of the ambient noise cleared, so that I can make out what it is saying.

OK. It's almost right. I just need to turn the volume up a little more...slow it down. See ghosts it sometimes don't have a concept of time, hence the reason why we need to speed the audio up or slow it down, which allows us to understand it better.

EVP, electronic voice phenomenon, occurs when a voice is captured that the human ear can't hear on an electronic device. However, our device is a voice recorder especially designed for this. This is what I love to analyze the most! I love this part of it, and it is always incredible to hear a ghost speak!

Well, we did catch a voice – and it's talking – fast! Slowing it down a bit more...almost...almost there...a little more, and... BINGO!

"Kevin come here and listen to this!" I said excitedly, while pulling the headphones off my head.

Headphones help block out other noises, and lets me concentrate better. Last time, I didn't wear them, and Kevin's bodily functions made more noise, which just kept me laughing. Yes, guys love to laugh at farts and burps. But a hard lesson learned? No chili, *before* an investigation.

As Kevin reached for the headphones, I reminded him to listen very closely to the audio. It is possible that years of Motley Crue, cranked up to the max, may have damaged Kevin's hearing. But, then, it could be because he has ADHD, and just doesn't pay attention. He put the headphones over his ears, and I could see him concentrate hard.

"Are you ready?" I asked him.

He looked at me with a dumfounded look, and he murmured, "You didn't start the audio yet?"

Welcome to my world. I put the clip on a loop, and hit play. Kevin cupped his hands around the earpiece, and looked at me with a smile.

"Dude, there's a guy saying 'get out'! How freaking cool."

"Yeah, Kev. That's what I heard, too. And, that file was pulled right after we found the jar."

"So, could it be Mrs. Davis' old man?"

"Couldn't tell you. But, it sort of fits. Who else would have said that?"

"Lucias Clay," said Kevin.

"Who?"

"You know the guy from the song?"

Yes, this is how my night is going to end. Kevin now is singing the full song, as I close up my laptop, and turn towards the bed. It's going to be one hell of a night.

11

After listening to the audio capture for hours, I finally climbed into bed around 5 o'clock, and slept for a few hours. I awoke to a rumbling sound that reminded me of an earthquake. With caution I opened my eyes to see Kevin sitting in his boxers, rubbing his big belly. I began to sit up, and smelled something that was very much like raw sewage. Kevin stood, and walked towards the bathroom, farting the whole way! He closed the door, and I covered my head with the blanket hoping to filter out the smell. About an hour later, and after the smell cleared the room, we were showered, dressed, and ready to go. We took the equipment off the chargers, and packed the bags. As I began to grab the door knob, someone knocked. I opened the door, and my mouth dropped. It was Jonathan, and he was dressed in a suit and tie!

"Good morning gentleman," he said with enthusiasm. "We ready to head out?"

"Dude! I need food, breakfast food, first! I can't hunt on an empty stomach," Kevin said, then added, "Is there anywhere that we can get some all you can eat pancakes?"

If I had a free hand, I would slapped myself silly – not once, but twice! So, when Jonathan said that he knew a place that had all you can eat pancakes, I was surprised.

We loaded the truck, and pulled out of the motel parking lot. Jonathan turned the radio off, so we could talk. However, for a long, awkward moment, there was silence.

"I just don't know how to ask," declared Jonathan, "but did you find any ghost things?"

"Well," I spoke up, "we did get an EVP of a man telling us to get out. It was faint, and having only one sound is not enough to prove anything. We went through hours of audio and countless pictures. Nothing else."

"So, do *you* think it was Lou Davis?" Jonathan asked me.

"Well, no one can be sure, because it's just a voice, and since we have never spoken to him, it's inconclusive. If I said that it was, we would be jumping to conclusions, and that would get us nowhere."

"Yeah," Kevin agreed, then added," If a ghost would say 'hey, yo! Over here! It's me, Lou!', then we could say it was him."

I turned to look at Kevin with amazement. His totally, obscured statement was just plain dumb! The sad thing was that Kevin was truly proud of his statement. I shook my head, and returned to staring out of the windshield.

"I totally understand, Kevin. I just was wondering how long till we can determine who or what is haunting the Davis' land. We don't have much time, and every minute counts."

"Jon, you need to understand that the paranormal isn't an exact science. We need as much time as it will take. If we could give you a time frame, we would, but it is an impossibility," I said. "Plus, we are here to prove a haunting, and to back up the claims. We know one thing. The voice said that there was money buried there. We found some."

"Obviously, but what is keeping people from actually finding it? Something is scaring that old lady, and if she can't get to the money, she loses everything. Her home, land, and every possession she owns. I can't let that happen."

"Even if we do find proof of haunting, how would the ghost keep others from finding all of it? Just ow would we keep those spirits away?" I added, "I have heard of ways, but we have never tried to get rid of a ghost, or to hold it back."

If we knew how to keep an angry spirit away, maybe Sam would still be here. Maybe we could save her, and the rest of the team.

"Leave that to me, Mike. I have been doing some research, and I think I may know of someone who could help," Jonathan told us. He continued, "I will make a call when we get there. But, first let's eat."

Jonathan turned into a little roadside café with a sign outside that said "all you can eat buttermilk pancakes".

I thought, *"Well, there goes another mom and pop joint going out of business, because of Kevin's massive appetite! Man! They don't know what they are in for."*

We exited the truck, and walked to the door. Kevin made it to the entrance first, of course. He moves quicker when food is involved.

We were seated by a woman who looked old enough to be my mother, but she was probably younger than me. I saw a pack of cigarettes in her apron, so I guess it's true that smOKing ages a person.

I looked through the menu, sitting in a chair opposite Jonathan and Kevin. Having chosen my breakfast, I lowered the small menu, and looked over Jonathan's shoulder through the big, plate glass window. Another bright day! Maybe we'll get lucky, and find the answers today.

12

The three of us walked into our room, and quickly started to eat. It was very noticeable that several legs were missing, as well as a few biscuits. Kevin made a hasty retreat from the table, before he could see our eye roll. He flopped on his bed, grabbed the remote, and turned on the TV, while Jonathan and I talked about, well, nothing really. Just small talk to help us wind down the day.

After Jonathan was finished, I cleaned the table, then replaced the food with my laptop. Kevin abandoned the TV, and began watching the videos. I downloaded the voice recorders. As I was going through them, I realized that the only one that had been recording was the one I had with me. Well, that certainly will save me some time.

I looked up to see Kevin pulling out lots of different cords, and by some strange miracle among all that mess, he found the right cords to connect the camcorder to the TV. While I knew we had them, who he would put two and two together, and find the right ones?

He stretched out on his bed to start the video, and I opened the audio file in a digital audio editing program that is installed on our computer. That way, I can use several different filters to help clarify any and all sounds that don't seem to fit with any other sounds.

I put on my headphones, and started playing the audio. It's really hard to find any odd noises outside, because most of the sounds that we hear are already odd, since we don't investigate in open air very much. So, I need to listen more carefully than I might normally would. I sat with my back to the TV and Kevin, so I am not distracted.

About an hour later, I feel something hit me on my back. I turned to see Kevin sitting on the edge of the bed frantically rewinding, and watching the same video continuously.

"What do you got Kev?" I was a bit cautious, but hoping for something exciting by what he might have found.

"Dude! I got a figure messing with the broken camera! It knocked down the tripod and moved away!" he exclaimed.

I ran to the bed, and sat next to him. And, sure as shit! There it is!! A figure stepped through the bushes, reached out to push the tripod over, then it turned and moved away!

"It's still hard to make out," I said. "But, there is no doubt that it's definitely a figure on the cam! And, it looks solid! I also found part of a footprint near the tripod in that area, too!"

"But, why couldn't we see this person while we were there? I mean, Dude! We would have known if someone was out there!"

"I don't know," I answered, "but this is a great find – either way!"

This is the first time that we have ever captured a full-body apparition before, so, I am not exactly sure how it is suppose to look. I figured that it should be kind of translucent, or maybe a part of a body. At least that is what I have seen on the internet. Most of those, though, I believe are fake.

The way this figure moves, it's a little clumsy, and doesn't look paranormal. But, Kevin was right. How could we not have known if someone was there? Well, no matter what, it sure looks like we got a mystery, Scooby Fans! But, will we be able to solve it?

After another few hours of video and audio work, we called it quits, and went to bed. Seeing Kevin in his boxers was weird enough, but watching him sleep with his trash bag? I won't even go into that one!

13

About an hour passed, and Kevin is sitting on the edge of the boat, while I have been standing by camera three. He stands and walks in my direction. We are trying to keep noise levelss down and to avoid getting in front of the cameras in order to film all the natural sights and sounds. If there *is* a change in these, we can easily see them during review.

We usually stay static for an hour or two. But, that usually happens when we investigate in an interior. It's a little harder outdoors. The biggest reason we are doing it here is that we don't want to row back and forth any more than necessary.

As Kevin approaches, I nod at him, and he smiles. As he comes closer to me, I get a whiff of chocolate? It's probably my imagination, because I am starting to get hungry. But, it is such a strong smell!

"What's up Mike?" Kevin asks.

"Nothing. Just standing and watching. See anything over there?" I asked.

"Nah. Just bugs bugging me," he answers.

This is weird, because I haven't seen any bugs around me. Nothing at all. In this clearing, it's as if we are in a huge bubble, where nothing is able to push its way in nor can anything exit. And, Kevin is complaining about bugs?

"Well, I think we should do a sweep, and then, check out what's on the other side of this tree line."

Kevin smiled,

"Good I was starting to get really bored over there."

We grabbed a voice recorder and EMF meter, before we walked around the clearing. No spikes like there were yesterday, and not a single sound. So, we made our way to the tree line, and pushed through the brush. The weeds are thick, and tangled together. In the distance, we see some really cool trees that are dripping with hanging moss.

The humidity starts to rise, the air becomes heavy with no breeze stirring, and it's getting hard to breathe. and Kev is panting behind me. I am having a hard time, but it may kill him.

Then, we enter a huge cold spot! The hair on my arms stand straight up. The EMF meter alarm rings, and Kevin watches the spike on the meter.

"Five point three mill gauss jump, and holding steady. Temp dropped seven degrees, and continues to fall!" Kevin exclaimed.

I double check to make sure the voice recorder is recording and start asking normal questions for responses. Kevin audibly announces any changes on the meter.

In addition, we are also discovering personal emotions, such as a calm feeling without one ounce of fear – almost like a child being in its mothers arms. If it wasn't for the cold, I would feel the best I have in months!

As the serenity surrounds us, we heard a loud scream, followed by a crashing sound. Something was moving through the brush, but we can't tell the direction. Also, we can't tell which way we came, and we realized that we are lost!

Whatever is moving in the brush seems to be circling us. While we can't see what it is, we are absolutely sure it's huge!

"Mike turn right, and go straight. Hurry!"

"Kev this way," I yell.

We start running through the overgrown bushes and weeds, and we run through the thorn bushes, we feel the thorns ripping through our skin as blood runs from the gashes! But, it doesn't stop us! Kevin runs past me, as if I was standing still. At least, he is clearing a path for me!

I could see an opening, and Kevin pushes towards it. He is only a few yards away, when he – disappears! I slow down to assess the situation, and realize that he stepped into a rabbit snare, which tripped him.

"Are you OK?" I asked, sighing with relief.

"Dude what the hell is that? Why would someone pull a stunt like that out here?" Kevin said, trying pull off the snare. Then, grinding his teeth, he continues. "Someone has a real bad sense of humor!"

I helped Kevin to a standing position, and we ran into the clearing. Uh-oh! One of our cameras has been knocked over, and of course, it is busted!

"Kevin, lets grab everything, and get the hell out of here!"

"You got it," Kevin said as he turned to go grab the first camera he put up.

I looked to where the camera was laying, and see a partial footprint? It looks a lot like the footprint I found earlier. And, it isn't really a shoe, but a work boot. So, I snapped several photos of it.

After I packed the broken camcorder, I started to break it down the other one, while thinking about everything that had happened so far. I hope that one of the other cameras picked up what happened to the fallen cam.

"All packed dude? Do you need help?" Kevin asked, as he walked towards me.

"No. I got it, "I responded. "What do you think is going on out here?"

"Dude! I don't know, but I think that an alligator was trying to hunt us down."

"Kevin that wasn't a gator," I said, rolling my eyes. He has to stop this! "Will you stop using the alligator as an excuse for making those noises?"

14

We carried our packed bags to the boat. As Kevin rowed, I kept looking back to see if anything else was strange. I could see nothing at all.

We were in the clearing for the better part of four hours. But, everything seemed to happen quickly, so, it felt as if four hours went by fast! Pulling out my phone, I blinked. Had time sped up somehow? I look at my phone, again. Finally, there was one bar, and that was just enough to call Jonathan to see where he was. He was having a glass of lemonade with Mrs. Davis. I told him we are on our way back, then I disconnected the phone.

When we reached shore, Mrs. Davis and Jonathan were walking down to meet us, and she hugged me as soon as she was near me.

"Thank you," she said to me. "That jar you found had over five hundred dollars in it!"

"I made a temporary deal with the bank for the money," Jonathan said. "Hope we can get someone over there soon to find the rest. So how did it go?"

"Still inconclusive," I answered. "Got more data to go over."

While we were talking, Kevin hauled the bags to Jonathan's Escalade and tossed them in the back. He then leaned into the back seat, and when he stood, we could see him chewing on something. I haven't eaten anything since breakfast, and I know that we didn't grab any food, before we left, so, what was he chewing on?

I am starting to feel more like a treasure hunter, than a paranormal investigator. Jonathan had stated earlier that he hoped to find the rest of the money soon. It irritated me a little bit. We are here to document anything we find that might be considered paranormal, and instead, we are looking for jars full of money!

Focus, Mike! We have hours of audio to listen to, and I can't be distracted. It takes four hours per voice recorder. Both Kevin and I need to concentrate. Hopefully, there will be something on it that will appear.

"Come on guys let's get moving, so that we can start reviewing. We got a lot of work to do, before we come back tomorrow," I said as I started to walk to the truck.

"Also," Kevin added, "we need to get some grind age."

"What's *grindage?*" Jonathan asked

"You know munchables, grub, chow, food. Pick one! I am *hungry* Jon."

All I thought was when isn't he hungry. So, we jumped into the truck, and stopped to pick up a couple of buckets of chicken with all the sides. That is when Jonathan realized that it's not wise to let Kevin order – *ever*!

We head to the Escalade with Kevin in tow, carrying the buckets. His face looked as if he had done something wrong. His mouth moved! That bugger stole a biscuit!

Driving away, Jonathan and I talked about what he expected from us. I made it extremely clear that we are *not* treasure seekers.

He assured me that all he wanted to know was if the area is haunted, and if something is truly guarding the stash of money. And, he explained that his hope is that we can find evidence from contacting a spirit about where the money might be hidden.

It was a short drive back to the hotel. We pulled into the lot and parked. As we got out of the truck, I noticed that my friend is covered in chicken breading. I just hope he left us something to eat!

15

The three of us walked into our room, and quickly started to eat. It was very noticeable that several legs were missing, as well as a few biscuits. Kevin made a hasty retreat from the table, before he could see our eye roll. He flopped on his bed, grabbed the remote, and turned on the TV, while Jonathan and I talked about, well, nothing really. Just small talk to help us wind down the day.

After Jonathan was finished, I cleaned the table, then replaced the food with my laptop. Kevin abandoned the TV, and began watching the videos. I downloaded the voice recorders. As I was going through them, I realized that the only one that had been recording was the one I had with me. Well, that certainly will save me some time.

I looked up to see Kevin pulling out lots of different cords, and by some strange miracle among all that mess, he found the right cords to connect the camcorder to the TV. While I knew we had them, who he would put two and two together, and find the right ones?

He stretched out on his bed to start the video, and I opened the audio file in a digital audio editing program that is installed on our computer. That way, I can use several different filters to help clarify any and all sounds that don't seem to fit with any other sounds.

I put on my headphones, and started playing the audio. It's really hard to find any odd noises outside, because most of the sounds that we hear are already odd, since we don't investigate in open air very much. So, I need to listen more carefully than I might normally would. I sat with my back to the TV and Kevin, so I am not distracted.

About an hour later, I feel something hit me on my back. I turned to see Kevin sitting on the edge of the bed frantically rewinding, and watching the same video continuously.

"What do you got Kev?" I was a bit cautious, but hoping for something exciting by what he might have found.

"Dude! I got a figure messing with the broken camera! It knocked down the tripod and moved away!" he exclaimed.

I ran to the bed, and sat next to him. And, sure as shit! There it is!! A figure stepped through the bushes, reached out to push the tripod over, then it turned and moved away!

"It's still hard to make out," I said. "But, there is no doubt that it's definitely a figure on the cam! And, it looks solid! I also found part of a footprint near the tripod in that area, too!"

"But, why couldn't we see this person while we were there? I mean, Dude! We would have known if someone was out there!"

"I don't know," I answered, "but this is a great find – either way!"

This is the first time that we have ever captured a full-body apparition before, so, I am not exactly sure how it is suppose to look. I figured that it should be kind of translucent, or maybe a part of a body. At least that is what I have seen on the internet. Most of those, though, I believe are fake.

The way this figure moves, it's a little clumsy, and doesn't look paranormal. But, Kevin was right. How could we not have known if someone was there? Well, no matter what, it sure looks like we got a mystery, Scooby Fans! But, will we be able to solve it?

After another few hours of video and audio work, we called it quits, and went to bed. Seeing Kevin in his boxers was weird enough, but watching him sleep with his trash bag? I won't even go into that one!

16

"Mike you must know the truth. Only the truth will get you through this. look for the print, and follow your heart. All is not what it seems. Only you can put the two together and one is the only real one."

The buzz of the alarm woke me up, and even though I felt cold, I was sweating. I could still hear the voice of Carrie, saying the same thing over and over. I sat up with those things still going through my head. Was it a dream or not? I stood, and walked to the table, where I began to write down everything that I heard. Dream or no, it may be important, I am neither a psychic, nor do I claim to be. However, Carrie was, and I hear her often. This might be part of her gift that I never knew about.

After finishing, I padded over to the bathroom. I passed Kevin who was still sleeping. OK. The temptation of needing to look into the huge garbage bag was over whelming. I made up my mind to look inside it, when Kevin started to stir, lost my nerve, and chided myself for being a coward, as I continued to the bathroom.

Fifteen minutes later, I was clean and refreshed. Kevin was bouncing around, doing the pee pee dance, and pushed past me as he ran into the bathroom. Wishing he would just close the door, I started to dress. Hearing his moans of relief was enough to pull my clothes on really fast, then I walked outside as fast as I could.

The air smelled clean, and it was quiet around the motel. There was a picnic table on the other side of the parking lot that was calling my name. Just a place to sit in peace beckoned me to think over all that is going on in my life.

I was deep in thought when Jonathan sat down next to me with three cups of coffee that he had in a carrier. He lowered the cup carrier to the table, pulling out two cups. Handing one to me, he half-heartedly said good morning. That is when I took a good look at him. He sure didn't look well. It looks like he didn't sleep at all.

"You OK, Jonathan?"

"Yeah. I just didn't sleep well. Every time I managed to doze off, a weird dream kept waking me up," Jonathan explained. "The dream seemed very real, and there was a guy in it that I had never seen before, who was telling me the same thing over and over."

"What did he say?" I asked him with curiosity.

" 'look behind the shed', was all he said to me. I have no clue what that means!"

"That's kinda weird. I do know that some people think that dreams are part of the mind that receives messages from beyond, or somewhere else." I paused and looked at him as he drank his coffee. "So," I asked, "what did this guy look like?"

Jonathan put his coffee down, cupping it with both hands, and began to tell me that he saw no real face. All he could really tell me was that the man was around six feet tall, and wore a hat. Anything other than that was too blurred.

I tried to get him to shake off the dream by changing the topic, and thankfully, he slowly started talking about other things. It's funny how some people take to heart everything that they have in a dream. We sat and talked, taking in the bright sunny day, when a loud sound interrupted our peace. Yes. It was what we feared! Kevin was heading our way. Here is a shock; he is wearing the same clothes for the third day.

"Dudes."

His greeting always left something to be desired. Next. He normally follows it up with some other disgusting, gassy sounds. But, this time, he just sat down. Jonathan handed him a cup of coffee. He pulled off the lid, and took his first sip. Then – he belched. Now, that is the Kevin I knew and loved.

"Dude you tell Jon Jon about what we caught?" Kevin blurted out in between sips.

"No Kevin I didn't, because I am not sure what or who it is, yet. But, since you brought it up... Jonathan, we got what looks to be a man knocking over one of our cameras. I don't know if it's human or not, but we definitely caught something!"

Jonathan looked shocked at my announcement. His head darted toward me, then to Kevin, who had a silly ass grin on his face, while he bounced up and down. He gave Kevin a double take, then looked back at me with a bewildered look on his face.

"You're telling me that you actually saw something knock over the camera and tripod. You're jOKing right?"

"No Jon we got something but before I show you I want to run it through a video editing program to clean it up some, and enlarge it so it will be easier to see. The cameras were set up far enough away from each other to capture as much space as possible," I told him, before I continued. "But, since the distance is so far away, you just see a dark figure and not much else. I do want to get back there and check on a few things, though."

Jonathan agreed with me, and we started to begin our day, when Kevin said something that stopped us mid step.

"I'm hungry. Aren't we going to breakfast, first?"

After rolling our eyes, again, and a quick stop a fast food place to grab some breakfast for Kevin, we headed to the swamp. Kevin took one of about everything in the sack (a really big surprise, I know), and ate as the three of us drove to see Mrs. Davis. Shockingly, he was done before we got there.

As we turned into the driveway, we saw Mrs. Davis lying on the ground. Jonathan slammed on the breaks, and we jumped out of the truck. There was a basket laying a couple feet away from her, and she was on her side. I got to her first, and asked if she was OK. She looked at me with a tear in her eye and said she tripped and fell. Asking if she needed an ambulance, which she turned down, we propped her up to a sitting position.

Mrs. Davis said something had gotten her attention, and she tripped over a root and fell. Then, she said she wasn't hurt, but couldn't get back to her feet. At that instance, she looked at me and thanked us for being there for her.

We helped her get to her feet, and she dusted herself off. Jonathan and I walked her back to her house, while Kevin grabbed the basket and followed.

She thanked us again, when we reached the door, and invited us in. Mrs. Davis then explained that she was going to the neighbors to buy some preserves to spread on some homemade bread she was planning on making today. Jonathan offered to drive her if she was up to it, and she agreed.

Luckily, she bounced back as if she was a kid who had fallen off their bike. Still insisting she was not hurt, she got up and went to her bedroom to change into some clean clothes. This is something I really hoped Kevin would finally do. He was getting a bit ripe!

Since she was changing we exited the house and went to the truck. Kevin grabbed the equipment I asked for and we started to map out a game plan for the day. The funny thing is that he brought his bag with and it seemed a lot smaller today. Still puzzling.

We grabbed our things, closed the back of the Escalade, and started towards Jonathan. He told us that he was going to drive Mrs. Davis down the road, and he would be back shortly.

After they left, we headed down to the swamp. Kevin swung his leg into the boat and stopped.

"look dude!" he said loudly, while pointing across the swamp to the clearing.

I could see what looked like a man jump into the bushes and disappear.

"Kev! lets get over there quick!"

We both sat down next to each other and started to row across the water to the clearing. Both of us were keeping an eye out for any other weird things to happen. All I keep thinking is someone is over there screwing with us, and this is all just a damn, big sham!

We ran the boat onto the land, grabbed our bags, and took off running toward the area where we saw the man. No footprints. No broken branches. Nothing at all to show that someone was there.

"Hey, Kev. Let's get into this brush to check out what's beyond this clearing. I have a feeling about it."

So, we started to break through the cover, and then, I wished I had something with me so I could cut a path. Not only was it covered with wild plants, but they intertwined with each other, making it impossible to move quickly.

"Dude. I got that survival knife with the equipment. Stay here, and I will go grab it," said Kevin. "Be right back."

He turned around and returned the same way we had come. I pulled a voice recorder out of my pocket, and hit record. Thinking this would be the best time to do a quick EVP session.

I asked a series of questions, giving a lengthy pause in between each. But all of a sudden, I realized that Kevin has been gone a while. I knew we were not that far into the brush, so I yelled out to him. The silence was deafening. After no response, I yelled out again. Still nothing.

I proceeded to follow our trail back to the clearing. Kevin wasn't there. Our boat wasn't there, but it was 20 feet out into the swamp! All that I saw was the equipment bag; wait Kevin had his bag with us too. What the hell was going on around here?

I continued to scan the area, calling out Kevin's name. But no responses. Trying to keep my cool, I searched around for any clues. Well, that didn't work. Now, I started to panic.

"The print," said a familiar voice.

I walked back to where the camcorder was set up the day before, and searched again for that footprint. Pushing away a little brush, I was surprised when I saw it right in front of me! It was still in the soft earth, and I looked up to see a path behind a small tree.

I had to run back to the equipment to grab a camcorder to document what I had seen. I gave one more yell for Kevin, before heading down the path. This was clearly man made. The branches were cut, so no animal could have done this.

I took my time heading into the unknown. I sure didn't want to fall and get hurt. I also had to find Kevin. Every few steps I took, I would look behind me to see how far the clearing was from my position. I didn't know the area, so there is a fear of getting lost.

After a bit, the clearing was out of view. Now, I needed to keep my senses open, and be aware of what is around me. The path was narrow, so, I figured if I stuck a branch in the path every twenty feet or so, I wouldn't get lost. Well, that was an idea they may have worked – *if* I did it every twenty feet, not every ten minutes. But, I still plugged on, while calling out Kevin's name once in a while.

I then stopped in surprise. Why hadn't I thought of that earlier?

"Crap! My cell phone!"

In this day of technology, sometimes, it just slips your mind. Well, good idea, but that was shot down. I had no bars. Disappointed, I slid my phone back into my pocket and moved on.

Out of nowhere, I heard the loud voice, again.

"Get out!"

It startled me, but I had to keep going. I have been told that many times before, and nothing ever happened.

"Go! Or, you will meet the same fate as your fat friend!"

OK. I am thinking that there isn't something paranormal going on after all.

And, how did I counter that? I yelled back, of course!

"I am leaving. Please, don't hurt me!"

I took a few steps off the path, and kept moving forward. Every few steps I looked to make sure that I am still heading the right way. After a while, I see another smaller clearing, and an old, small building was smack in the middle. I peeked through the brush to see that someone was digging holes all over. Pretty obvious. looking for the money.

To the right of the building, I see an old shoe that I recognized. It was Kevin's shoe, lying in the middle of the clearing. With the entire tree covering the clearing, it is really shady with just a hint of sunlight. Then, I remembered the camcorder. So, I held it up, and hit record. I reached into my pocket, and pulled out my phone to check the time. Well, time flies when you're having fun, and dusk is coming very fast.

I put the phone back into my pocket, and knelt down. I watched the door to the building open, and Clay walked out of it. Through binoculars he scanned the area, and turned and walked back into the building, shutting the door behind him. And, this time, I have it on film!

Not far away from me, there was a stump that was pretty flat. So, I made my way to it, and set the camcorder on it. Luckily, it had a great view of that door .so it will record everything that happens.

You know outside of the paranormal, I am not really a brave man. This kind of scares me a bit. Does he have a gun or maybe a knife? Does he have Kevin and is he alive?

Well, suck it up buttercup, and you got to do something. I start towards the building, and I see a shovel leaning against the side. OK, if Clay does anything, I will come out swinging.

As I carefully walk to the building, I hear someone talking loudly. I can't make out what he is saying, but it's the same voice I heard telling me to get out of the area. I grab the shovel like a baseball bat and take a couple practice swings.

Now that I feel like I could hit a homer, I walk around to the door. Should I knock? Now, that's stupid. I know I will yell. and he will come running out. Except that my first try came out like a squeak. OK. Deep breath.

"HEY!" I yelled.

18

The door shot open, and Clay came rushing out. I swung the shovel, missing him, and hit the building. Something fell off from above, and hit Clay in the head, knocking him to the ground. Well, at least it worked.

I stepped over Clay's unconscious body so that I could look inside. I saw Kevin hog tied and gagged. He was in his boxers – which reminded me to stop at the store, and pick up some bleach. His clothes were in a pile next to him, and his garbage bag was on the table. Finally, I could see what was inside it.

I walked over to Kevin, and untied him. As he pulled off the gag, I looked into the bag to see…junk food? What the hell? There were candy, chips, and Twinkies. I love Twinkies.

"Dude! That crazy old dude clobbered me on the back of my head!"

"Are you hurt Kev?" I asked.

"Well, got me a killer headache, but I'm good."

I turned to see Clay who was starting to move. I walked towards him.

"You OK?" I asked him.

"Yeah," he answered, sitting up and rubbing his head.

"Clay...you want to explain all of this? What in the hell are you doing?"

"I want my money. Lou took all our money, and hid it somewhere. I kept everyone out of here for a long time. Then you three came. And, I couldn't scare you off."

I helped the old man to his feet, and saw Kevin emerge from the building fully dressed. I had a good hold of Clay, so he wouldn't get away. But, then I saw something I couldn't believe. Standing at the edge of the brush was a man, well half of a man, floating toward us.

Clay saw him screamed and yanked his arm out of my grasp. I tried to grab him, again, but missed. Clay sprinted down the path with Kevin running after him. I ran to get the camcorder off the stump to capture everything. I turned to see if I could film the apparition, but it wasn't there.

I caught up to Kevin and Clay in the clearing near our equipment bag. Both were out of breath and gasping for air. Still holding the camera I turned and did a three sixty to scan the area.

"Who or what was that Clay and why are you running?" I demanded.

"Its Lou! C-can't you see him?" he stammered in fear.

I looked around, and still saw nothing. Now, I am second guessing what I saw, and I never second guess. I sure hoped I got it on video. Clay became upset when we saw nothing. It took some time, but Clay finally calmed down. How could we get the boat back so we could leave? It is halfway into the swamp, and there really might be alligators out there. Suddenly, I realized something.

"Clay, how did you get out here? You have a boat, or something, that will get us back to the house?" I asked

"Yeah it's over there. It's in a duck blind. Surprised to see you're as dumb as the damn ducks! You passed it every time you came out here!" he said with a snicker.

Well, he was right! Sure as shit, we never saw it, or even paid attention to what was around us! It had been dragged to drier ground, and covered with branches and hay. It was truly camouflaged. To me, it still looks like a huge bush, even though I know what it is.

The three of us walked to the boat, and Kevin started to clear off the excess branches and limbs. There was even a small battery powered motor on it. Although Kevin was cleaning it off, there was still a lot on the boat.

"Clay, climb in! We are heading back to the house," I ordered. "Kev grab the bags, get in, and I'll push us off."

I tried to push the boat into the water a bit, while Kevin loaded the boat. But it wouldn't move, because the ground was so soft, the boat, slowly, began to sink.

Kevin saw that I was having some trouble, because I was still holding onto the camcorder. He walked around to give me a hand. When we were finished, we got the boat moving to the edge of the swamp. But, as we did we heard the buzz of the trolling motor.

Before we could jump into the boat, Clay put the boat into reverse, and pulled away from shore. Kevin, with all his wit, dove into the swamp to try and reach the boat. Well, he tried anyway. Instead, did a belly flop!

I watched Clay turned the boat around, and started to move forward. At that time, the boat stopped, suddenly, drifting about thirty feet from the shore. Frantically, Clay was trying to get the motor to work.

At the bow of the boat, the floating figure reappeared. And, it was moving towards Clay. When he saw it, he started to yell. He kept moving towards the back of the boat, until he fell over the edge. The floating figure was watching as it "stood" mid boat. Then, it made its way back to the stern, and followed Clay into the water.

We watched as Clay tried to keep his head above water, reaching for the boat. He was inches away, and with a blood curdling scream, he repeated the same words. He was yelling over and over.

"He has me! He has me!"

Was Clay thinking that it was Lou pulling him down under the swamp?

All we could do was stand there and watch, while Clay was pulled down into the calm water. And, he never surfaced!

Kevin walked out of the waist deep water, soaked from head to toe. I knew that it was the first time that those clothes seen water in a while. He shook his feet, when he exited the water, and moved across the soft ground.

"Dude! I tried!' he exclaimed.

"I know Kev. I still haven't seen Clay come up, yet. And, I don't think he will," I told him.

"Yeah what a way to go…now he is gator food," Kevin muttered, still shaking off swamp water. "It's a good thing you got it on video, because no one will ever believe this crap!"

I looked down to my hand, and the camcorder was still recording. Hopefully, I caught it. I turned the camera off, and hung my head low.

To be honest, I am really starting to hate death. I keep seeing people die, and that is not something that someone wants in their life. But, I needed to gain my composure, and try to figure a way back to the house.

I reached into my pocket for my cell phone, and looked for a signal. Yes! I have two bars. I sent Jonathan a text, and got a response immediately. Then, looking to the other side of the shore, I saw Jonathan. He had witnessed everything.

Jonathan assured me that he was getting help to get us back across the swamp. After his last text, I watched him leave. We were going to have some time while we waited. So, I decided to look around the shed, and see if I can find out why Clay was doing all of this. I mean, he is trying to scare Mrs. Davis into leaving and losing her property.

I asked Kevin to follow me back to the small clearing. If you have never been in a swamp before, you wouldn't know that the smell of methane was always around. Now, Kevin smelled like the swamp, too! Oh, crap! It's going to be so much fun, riding back to the motel with him.

We returned to the shed. Kevin went inside, as I walked around it. When I came to the back, I remembered something. The weeds were overgrown, but I pushed them aside to see the exterior better.

At he bottom, there was a wood plank that was not brand new, but not as rotten as the rest. I looked around it. I reached down, and gave a little tug. The nails easily pulled out of the stud.

I looked around, and found another small piece of wood that I could get in the small crack, which I stuck into it. Luckily it worked.

I saw a canvas bag. I grabbed it, and pulled it out. I then realized there were more inside! At least ten bags were inside, and I pulled them all out and laid them onto the ground. I opened one. I was money…*a lot* of money.

I yelled for Kevin, and he rushed around the building. The sound of his wet sneakers almost made me giggle. But, holding my composure, I showed him what was in the bag. After looking inside, he looked up at me and smiled.

"Looks like the cash wasn't buried in jars, but hidden in the walls of the shed, Kevin!" I told him with a big smile.

"Dude! I guess Mrs. Davis will be able to save her land after all!"

19

We pulled bag after bag out of the shed – all with money inside. Then, a cold chill came over my body! I have felt this before, many times. A spirit is near us. The hairs on my arm were standing up as the static charge became more apparent. And, along with it, a little fear crosses my mind, knowing what just happened to Clay. I tried to stay calm, when I looked at Kevin.

Kev isn't staying as calm as I am. When I looked over, he is leaning back on his hands, and his mouth wide. I turned to look behind me. The figure we had seen earlier was standing in front of us. Was this really Lou?

The figure is undoubtedly an older man with gray hair and a beard, wearing a button down shirt and maybe jeans? Hard to tell at this point. He looks soaking wet. looking down, I noticed that he had one leg, and the other foot is about three inches above the ground. Surprise gripped me when he spoke!

"I knows who ya are, and ya best give that there money to my wife. If ya don't, I will pull ya down like I did my thievin' brother! That son-of-a-bitch been tryin' to find my stash for years!" he told me. Then he continued. "Then, when he asked me where it were, I wouldn't tell him. That's when he knocked me out, and threw me in my own, damn swamp. I was a hundred feet from my house, and couldn't tell my wife! And, then, Clay kept scarin' her pretendin' to be some 'spook'. But, she stayed away from the water, and I couldn't get a-hold of him. She knew I spent time in that there shed, and she would have come here, and found the money. Clay was never too smart, and I once said I would bury the money to keep him away."

"Like that song," Kevin said, which quieted him down right away. You know what they say about curiosity, but he just had to ask. "So, Dude...how come you were able to grab him today?"

"He carried an iron cross with him. When I pushed the branch off the roof of the shed, he dropped it. While he carried it, I couldn't even get near him! But, now he's gone, and I can finally rest in real peace!"

I remember hearing that ghosts and iron don't mix. That's why all cemeteries have wrought iron fences. They serve to keep the wandering spirits inside. Guess it's true.

Lou's ghostly figure turned, and started to float away. Still thinking he is still not at peace, I had to ask him one last thing.

"Hey, Lou!" He turned to look at me. "Lou, why didn't you tell your wife? Why didn't you go to the house?"

His figure floated back to me.

"Years ago, I buried iron rails around the house. I feared that some of my past would come spook me. All it did was keep me from my house and wife," he explained. "Now, it is time for me to go."

The figure of Lou once again, turned and floated away. After a few seconds, his image disappeared. Soon there was no sign of Lou at all, and the temperature returned to a humid heat.

"Rest in peace, Dude!" Kevin called after him. "And, you could say something to your wife on this recorder, if you want!"

Kevin held up the voice recorder, and turned it on. He was just hoping that Lou would leave a message. I, on the other hand, was very doubtful.

I turned back to the shed and pulled even more bags out. There were far too many bags for the two of us to move at once. So, we would take some, and tell Jonathan where to get the rest.

We moved back to the opening where the equipment was sitting, and dumped the bags of money on the ground. Kevin plopped down on the ground with the bags. I, on the other hand, heard a sound of a prop plane. I started to look in the sky for it.

I didn't see anything, although it seemed to get closer and closer. Then as my neck was starting to hurt, the sound turned into splashing water. Turning, I saw a swamp, air boat pull up by the boat.

Jonathan jumped off the air boat, and walked toward the shoreline across the water. The air boat had two men in it. One jumped into the swamp, and tied a rope to our boat. The other end was attached to the air boat. I watched as one guy hit the throttle, pulling our boat to our side of the swamp. When it hit the shore, it finally slowed down, and turned back to the water.

The guy in our boat jumped out of it, and ran to the air boat, untying the two. He ran to us, and handed me the rope.

"Here are your keys, boys. Hope ya don't lose your boat again!" he said, and ran back to join his buddy.

The other guy hit the throttle, again, and we were hit by a strong gust of air from the massive propeller as they hit the water, picking up speed, and soon, were out of sight. I didn't even get to thank them.

Kevin stood, and started to load the boat. I stood as far back from him as possible, because he kind of smelled like a wet fart. Eventually, though,

I grabbed some bags to help him load the boat. Kevin stepped in and sat in the middle of the boat, as I pushed the boat from the shore into the water. I jumped in and Kevin rowed across the water. I was tired, and Kevin was in deep need of a shower and new clothes. But, we were both in a good mood. More importantly, we were able to help Mrs. Davis.

But then Kevin spoke.

"Dude! Would it of been cool if Lou said something like, 'You must go to the Dagobah system'."

Cool? Kill me now.

20

Jonathan stood on shore as we pulled our boat into shore. He helped pull us onto the bank, and I jumped out to help pull too. Jonathan laughed as he told us that he turned the wrong way, and found two guys with a still. They thought he was a cop, and he asked if they had a boat. We all had a huge laugh about it.

I told him we found money, and there is much more in the shed. He opened a bag, and looked inside. He took the bag, and ran up to the house to show Mrs. Davis, while we followed with the rest of them.

Mrs. Davis had obviously been watching, and slammed the screen door, running toward us. Wrapping her arms around me, she thanked me at least twenty times. After she let go of me, she moved towards Kevin with open arms, and stopped them.

"You smell like shit boy!" she told him.

I just couldn't help laughing hard, my stomach hurt. And, at the same time Mrs. Davis ordered Kevin to go into the bathroom and take a shower, while she washed his clothes.

"With soap!" she called after him.

I just laughed a lot harder. Kevin dropped the bags, and walked to the house slowly. She followed him to make sure he did what she had told him to do. I put the bags on the porch, and looked back to the swamp. It now looks so peaceful. Kevin shattered that peace when he busted through the door, again.

"Dude! I forgot the voice recorder! Can you hold on to my wallet?"

Still feeling in the backwoods moment, I sat on one of the porch stairs. I put Kevin's wallet down next to me, and looked on the voice recorder screen. One file for three minutes. Well, that isn't long, so I hit play.

I heard Kevin say that Lou could leave a message. It was then I thought I was hearing things! After hearing it once, I had to hear it, again! Just as it was finishing, Jonathan walked out of the house, carrying two beers, and sat down next to me.

I grabbed a beer, and explained what an EVP was, again, and told him that we caught the most impressive voice we had ever recorded. Jonathan asked me to play it.

"Mary-Ellen, my angel. I am sorry I am not there with ya, and I miss ya very much. Those boys found our money, and they are supposed to give it to ya.. This will make the rest of your days easy. Pray for me, as I think I am not going to be with

you, again. My past was not one that would make me an angel. But, you always shown the way of the lord. Love ya, and keep me in your heart."

A little background noise, and then, the recorder stopped. The look on Jonathan's face was priceless. I guess he had never heard an EVP before, because he hit me with tons of questions. And, I answered every one of them.

Kevin walked onto the porch wrapped in a blanket. I really shudder to think, but he probably doesn't have any clothes on underneath.

We played the audio for Kevin, and he had a grin from ear to ear. He kept saying, I told ya! I told ya, while he jumped around. Now, I don't want to scare anyone by repeating this, but a naked fat man wrapped in a small blanket, jumping around is not a pretty sight. Jonathan finally had enough, and jumped off the stairs forcing Kevin to settle down.

We then shared that clip with Mrs. Davis, which brought her to tears. It was hard to say if they were from sorrow or happiness. Either way, it gave her some closure, and that could mean a lot. Jonathan wrapped an arm around her, and took her back inside.

Later, Mrs. Davis shared stories about their lives. It seemed that she was taking everything fairly well.

Kevin's clothes were finally out of the dryer, and he was dressed. We said our goodbyes, and headed for Jonathan's Escalade.

We stopped for food and gas, while Kevin got a twelve pack of beer. We headed back to the motel, where the three of us talked and drank. I guess you can say we were celebrating.

In midst of the partying, I decided to ask Kevin about all his stash of food.

"Kev, was food the only thing you brought?"

"Yeah, but the old guy took it, and ate most of what was left. Then, we left the rest behind," he pouted a bit.

"But, why didn't you bring other things. Like, say...a change of clothes?" I asked.

"We didn't have room in the truck, I guess."

That big truck, and he didn't have room? He needed to do better than that.

"There was plenty of room," I said.

Kevin took a big gulp of beer.

"Dude, you said pack light. The snacks were almost ten pounds!"

I give up, I just can't even ask why he didn't share. Perhaps it's time for me to stop trying to understand Kevin.

"At least we didn't get pulled down in the swamp like the song," Kevin declared. Then, continued. "But poor Clay did, and he didn't even find the money."

Kevin was really strange, but he was always there for me. Plus, he was right about the song all along. Maybe I underestimate him? Nah!

21

After a couple hours, and a few beers, we all got some much needed sleep. For the first time in a while, I fell asleep fast. Must have been all the beers.

"You did good Mike."

This dream felt like it was real, and I had questions this time. Carrie will answer them without any riddles, or have me chase my tail around till I find out.

"Carrie, why didn't you just tell me where the money was? It would have made things easier."

"Have you made things easy for me? Ever? Plus, you're a smart person, and believe it or not, there are rules on this side. I can't just tell you everything. You need to find and grow as a person."

"Carrie, do I have a gift like you did. Is that how we can talk, and you can save me?"

"Mike your gift is me. Just like when I was alive, I can communicate with the other side. Just know we all look over you."

"Sam too? I need to know if Sam is near. I miss her, and knowing what happened to her haunts me every day."

"No she hates you, and is now hanging out with Kurt Cobain," she said. That isn't what I

wanted to hear, and sadness overwhelmed me. "You dumbass! Of course, Sam checks up on you. And, yes she misses you, and loves you still. What you did for that old lady made us all very proud. NOW WAKE UP AND BE A MAN!"

With that my eyes opened, and I jolted out of the bed with a lot of energy! The alarm was going off, and we were going to be heading home, soon. But, I just couldn't get the thought that Sam was still around me. And...she was proud of me! I was proud of us too.

I looked over to see Kevin's bare ass peeking out from under the cover. I shook my head. He would never change, and that was a slight bit of comfort. We all started this business to help people, and I feel like we finally have.

Unlike a week earlier, I know my purpose, now.

And, I know who I am.

I am Mike Taylor, and I am a ghost hunter.

About the author

Jason was born and raised in a suburb outside of Chicago. Living mainly with his father and grandmother after the age of ten, he was a normal kid. Not that great of a student, he made his way through high school, and finally graduated.

He tried living the rock and roll life style into his mid twenties, then decided to go back to school. At that time, he decided to go to a trade school instead of college. A counselor told him he had a form of dyslexia, and it could be the biggest reason he did poorly. Throughout school, he did rather well, scoring in the top five percent of his class.

But, that did not last long. He felt he was learning more in his trade working than at school. So, he dropped out to pursue his work. Many hits and misses came through his life ,but he battled through them all.

At the age of twent-seven, he lost his best friend – his Father. He felt alone and lost. Within the next three years, he married, and had two beautiful daughters.

The marriage didn't last, and he was on his own, again. After learning how to drive a truck, he felt like his life was finally getting better. Then another blow to him He injured his back, which changed his life.

Not being able to drive a truck anymore, he elected to go through with back surgery. As he was being put under, Jason stopped breathing. He discovered, later that he was allergic to penicillin. After Jason found out the surgery was a bust, and he nearly died, he decided to change his life.

Although he believes in the paranormal, he did not think he had ever had any near death experiences. But, his interest heightened. And after meeting his present wife, they both started investigating.

Now living in Moline, IL, and Jason still wanted to improve himself. He began writing about the paranormal for the most part. He, now, takes some of his experiences and cases, and writes fiction.

With dyslexia still in his path, he works forth and continues to battle against the odds.